what is happening
in the pictures.

Each child is an
individual and
develops at his
own pace.
Be patient
if your child
is struggling
with words.
It is more
important
to value what
he *can* do than to
become anxious about
progress. The learning
steps will all be taken in time, with your
help. At the back of this book you will find
suggestions on how to make the
best and fullest use of
this book.

* In order to avoid the clumsy 'he/she', the child is referred to as 'he'.

Geraldine Taylor is a national broadcaster, writer and authority on involving parents in their children's education. She contributes on this subject regularly to magazines for parents.

Working with schools in Avon, Geraldine helps parents and teachers to act in partnership to benefit children's learning confidence and family happiness.

Acknowledgment:
Front endpaper and cover illustrations by Lynn Breeze.

British Library Cataloguing in Publication Data
Taylor, Geraldine
  Talkabout baby.
  1. English language. Readers—For pre-school children
  I. Title   II. Skipworth, Richard   III. Bartlett, Amanda
  428.6
  ISBN 0-7214-1121-5

First edition
Published by Ladybird Books Ltd Loughborough Leicestershire UK
Ladybird Books Inc Auburn Maine 04210 USA
Printed in England

talkabout

baby

written by GERALDINE TAYLOR

illustrated by
RICHARD SKIPWORTH and AMANDA BARTLETT

Ladybird Books

There will be a new baby in the family soon...

Say hello to these new babies.
Who has come to see them?

Babies need lots of sleep...

...but sometimes they wake up at night.

Can you help to look after the baby?

It's bathtime!

Which belong to baby?

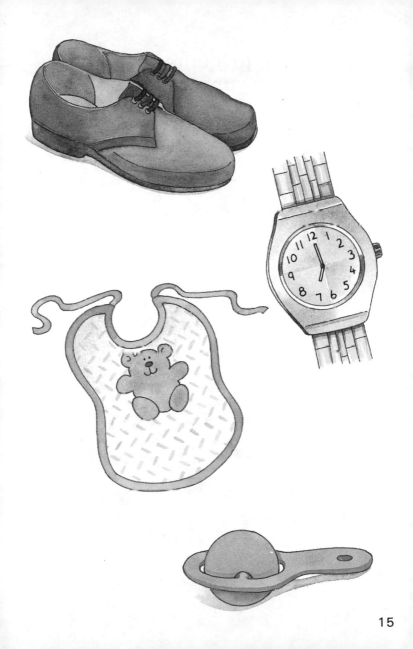

Babies have favourite things.
Can you remember yours?

It's washing day.
Look at all the colours!

What's happening in the picture?
Can *you* find these things?

Going out with baby.

Babies love to watch you.

What can this baby see?

Babies like exploring!

27

Can you tell the story?

Talk about these babies.
What are they doing?

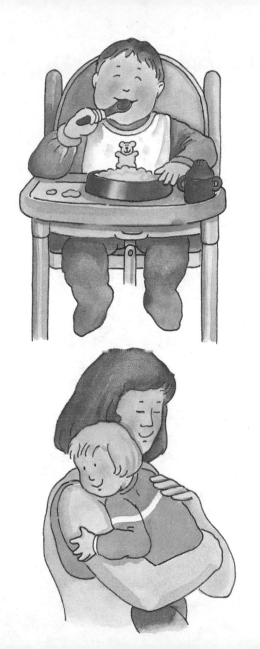

What's happening at the baby clinic?

Making baby smile!
What makes
you laugh?

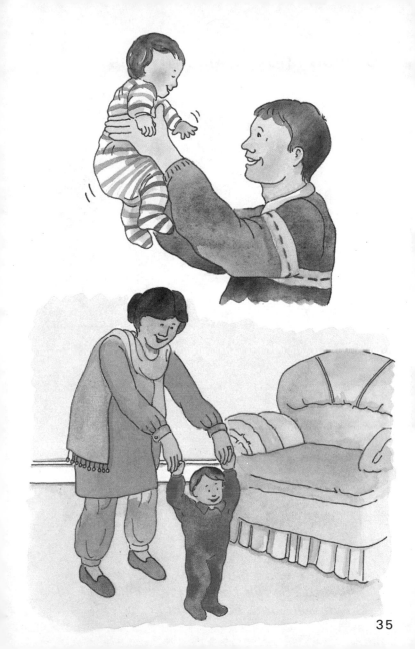

Do you know these rhymes?

Rock-a-bye baby, on the tree top.
When the wind blows the cradle will rock;
When the bough breaks the cradle will fall,
Down will come baby, cradle and all!

Pat-a-cake, pat-a-cake, baker's man,
Bake me a cake as fast as you can;
Pat it and prick it and mark it with B,
Put it in the oven for baby and me.

Babies grow up!

①

④

Can you tell the story?

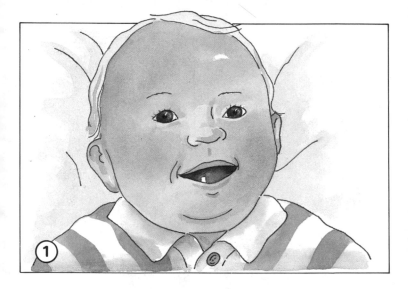

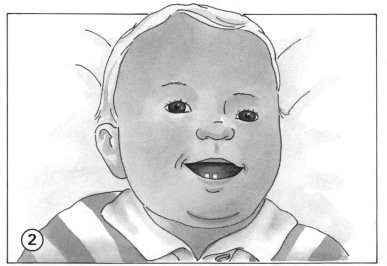

Time for bed!
Is it *your* bedtime yet?

Ten little fingers, ten little toes,
Two little ears, one little nose.
Two little eyes – they shine so bright,
One little mouth to kiss goodnight.

talkabout

talkabout baby

Toddlers and young children eagerly join in the excitement which surrounds the preparations for a new baby. Once the baby is born, though, things may not be quite as they expected!

The text and illustrations in **talkabout baby** are carefully planned to help prepare children for a new baby, to encourage them to get involved and to feel just as loved and included.

If your baby is to be born in hospital, it's especially important to explain who will be looking after the rest of the family. Reassure your child that you will not be away for many days and that you will be looking forward to his coming to see you and the baby in hospital.

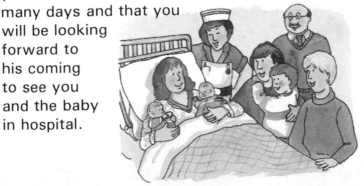